Harry the Homeless Puppy

Harry the Homeless Puppy

by Holly Webb

Illustrated by Sophy Williams

tiger tales

For Robin and William

tiger tales

5 River Road, Suite 128, Wilton, CT 06897
Published in the United States 2015
Originally published in Great Britain 2009
by Little Tiger Press
Text copyright © 2009 Holly Webb
Illustrations copyright © 2009 Sophy Williams
ISBN-13: 978-1-58925-474-9
ISBN-10: 1-58925-474-0
Printed in China
STP/1000/0085/0216
10 9 8 7 6 5 4 3 2

For more insight and activities, visit us at www.tigertalesbooks.com

Chapter One

"Beth, we need to go now," her dad told her gently. They didn't have much time before they needed to leave for the airport.

Beth didn't answer. She just stroked Harry's soft white head and chestnut-brown ears. She couldn't stop the tears from rolling down her cheeks. The puppy jumped up, placing his paws on her shoulder, and licked them away. "Oh, Harry, I'm going to miss you so much. I don't want to say good-bye," she whispered.

Her voice was so sad that Harry's curly tail stopped wagging. What was Beth talking about? It didn't sound good. He hoped they could leave this place soon. It was too noisy, and it smelled odd. There seemed to be a lot of other dogs here; he could hear them barking and growling and whimpering. He wanted to go back to his nice home.

"Here's his basket, and his toys," Beth's mother said, putting them into the cage. "I'm sorry, but we really do need to go, Beth; we have to go to the airport soon. It's going to be so exciting, isn't it?"

Harry watched his basket, his favorite red rubber bone, and squeaky fish being put into the wire cage. Beth squeaked the fish for him a couple of times, then rubbed her hand across her eyes. Harry gave a puzzled whine, looking up at Beth with his big brown eyes. What was going on?

"Oh, Mom, he knows something bad is happening," Beth said, as she got to her feet.

"Don't worry," the girl from the animal rescue shelter said gently. Her name was Sally and she seemed nice, but Beth wished she'd never had to meet her. "He'll find a good home really soon, I'm sure. He's such a sweet little dog. Puppies are always easy to find homes for, and Jack Russells are a popular breed."

Beth nodded, wiping her tears away with her sleeve. She supposed she should be glad about that — she certainly didn't want Harry to be here at the shelter forever, all miserable in a little cage. But she didn't want anyone else to have him, either! He was hers.

She'd only had him for two months,

when her dad broke the news to her that his company was sending him to Britain for three years. At first it had seemed so exciting, going to live in London, but almost at once she'd thought of Harry. Would he like it there?

And then Dad had said Harry couldn't come. That it would be too difficult with quarantine, and they would be living in a city apartment that wouldn't be suitable for a dog. Harry had to stay behind, and since they had no one to leave him with, he had to go to the shelter — a home for unwanted dogs. Which didn't seem fair, because Beth did want him, very much.

"We'll write to you to let you know when Harry's settled with a new owner," Sally promised. "Really soon. I know he's going to find a wonderful home."

Beth wanted to shout out that he had a wonderful home, but she nodded, and her dad led her out, which was good, because she was crying so much she couldn't see.

Harry whimpered, calling after her and scratching at the wire door. Beth was crying! There was something wrong, and she was going away from him. He howled for two hours, and then he was so exhausted he fell asleep.

When he woke up, she still hadn't come back.

"Oh, just look at this one," Grace said longingly. "A Labrador. Isn't she beautiful?"

Mom smiled at her. "We don't have the room, Grace, you know that. Even though she is beautiful. Such pretty eyes."

"Maybe a small dog, like a Jack Russell, then!" Grace started frantically scanning through the shelter website to see if they had any smaller dogs. "They're those cute little terrier dogs that used to hunt rats. They're really clever. And small! We've got room for one of those, definitely." Grace looked hopeful.

"No, we don't. And you'll need to get off the computer soon, Gracie, because I have to get on to the real estate website again, and see if any more apartments have come up." The Winters were looking to move at the moment, because there just wasn't enough room for them all in their current apartment, especially now that Grace and her brother, Danny, were getting older.

"It's no use, Gracie." Danny sighed, as he squeezed behind the computer chair to make some more toast. The computer was squashed into one corner of the kitchen. "I've been trying to convince Mom and Dad to get a dog for years."

Mom frowned at him. "Don't you start, Danny. You both know we just don't have the space. It's not fair to shut a dog up in an apartment, even a little dog. And definitely not on the seventh floor!"

Grace nodded. She knew it really, but every so often she managed to convince herself it wasn't true, just for a minute.

She went back to stirring her cereal, imagining running through the park with a beautiful black Labrador or a bouncy little brown-and-white Jack Russell scampering beside her. If they were moving anyway.... Was it too much to hope for a house with a yard? She licked her spoon dreamily.

"Don't get food on the keyboard, Grace!" Mom warned.

"Hey!" Danny had paused behind Grace's chair with his plate of toast, and was leaning over her shoulder. "Gracie, look! Mom, come and see!"

"I'm never going to get on my computer," Mom muttered, coming over to look at the screen. "Fairview Animal Rescue Shelter. You're still on the dogs' home website? Danny, haven't we all just agreed we can't have a dog?"

"Yes, but look. Our Fantastic Volunteers! People who help at the shelter." He grabbed the mouse and clicked on the link. "Look, they get to walk the dogs!" Danny beamed at Grace. "We could do that, couldn't we? I know we can't have our own dog, but we could borrow some. It would be like having lots of dogs!"

Grace practically pushed her nose up against the screen. There was a big photo of a hopeful-looking dog, with a leash in its mouth. Bonnie was her name, apparently. "Could we do it, Mom?" she asked eagerly. "The shelter's not far from here. Only a couple of streets away, on the other side of Fairview Park."

"Sounds like a good idea to me."
Dad had walked in, and was staring
at the computer now, too. "Anything
that gets you out in the fresh air and
not watching TV is good news. Does
it say when they're open? I'll take you
over there later, if you'd like."

Danny scanned the page. "We're always looking for more volunteers," he read. "Please drop by the shelter!"

Grace smiled up at Dad delightedly. "You really mean it?" she breathed. She hadn't really expected to be allowed a dog, and this was much, much better than nothing!

Harry was lying in his basket, with his nose shoved firmly into his blue cushion. It smelled like Beth's house — his house — and it shut out the smells of other dogs. He couldn't understand why Beth had left him here, and why she hadn't come back. Beth had brushed him and fed him and loved him. She had run into the house to find him and play with him as soon as she got home from school. What had gone wrong? He hadn't been naughty, he was sure.

He could still hear the other dogs barking and whining, no matter how hard he tried to bury his head in the cushion. But then he heard the sound of footsteps. Slowly, he crept out of his basket, and went to peer through the wire door of the cage. Maybe Beth was coming back. She might even be waiting for him out there! He sprang up against the wire hopefully, and from further up the corridor Sally turned around to look at him.

"Hey, Harry…," she said very gently. "You decided to come and see what's going on, did you?"

Harry's ears went back, and his tail sagged again. Beth wasn't there. Just that woman, Sally, who smelled like other dogs. He slunk back to his basket, and Sally sighed. She hoped Harry wasn't going to have a really hard time.

Harry thought miserably about home. It felt like now was the time he'd normally be curling up at the end of Beth's bed. His basket was usually only for daytime naps; he always slept with Beth. She'd probably have given him one of his favorite bone biscuits, too. He sighed, and snuffled sadly. She would come back, wouldn't she?

Chapter Two

Grace and Danny went to school around the corner from each other, Grace at the elementary school and Danny at the high school. So Danny usually walked Grace home, except on Tuesdays when Grace had ballet. But today, Mom was meeting them so they could all go to the animal rescue shelter, and sign up to be volunteers.

They'd gone on Saturday, but it had been really busy, and the staff had asked them to come back during the week so they could meet the dogs when everything was less hectic.

"Oh, where is she?" Grace swung her school bag impatiently.

"She's not even late yet! We were finished early for once," laughed Danny. "Hey, which dog do you want to take out? I really liked that big Golden Retriever on the website. He was great — I bet he runs like the wind!"

Grace smiled. "I don't care. Any of them. Oh, look, there's Mom!" Grace ran over to her. "You took forever! Can we go right there?"

Mom laughed. "Yes, but I just want to stop at the supermarket for a few things, okay?" She winked at Danny.

"Mo-om!" Grace's expression was tragic.

"She's kidding, Gracie!" said Danny. "Honestly, you're so gullible. Come on, let's get going."

Grace, Danny, and Mom stood in the rescue shelter reception area waiting for Sally, the manager, who was going to show them around. There was a constant noise of dogs barking and howling.

"You get used to it after a while," Mandy the receptionist said, smiling. "Think how happy you'll be making them, taking them out for walks. And it's not only walking. With some of the dogs it's just about companionship, a little playing or petting. I'm afraid some of them have been badly treated, and we need to help them to trust people again."

"But none of them is dangerous?" Mom asked anxiously. "I wouldn't like Danny or Grace to be with any dogs that might bite."

"No, no." The receptionist shook her head. "Volunteers only take out dogs that we trust completely." She grinned at them. "The only thing you need to worry about is not getting too attached! I've got three dogs from here, the ones I simply couldn't resist! You just have to remember that all the dogs are going to be adopted eventually, or we hope so anyway. So don't let yourselves get too fond of them, okay?"

Grace peeked through the glass door, looking at the dogs peering back at her from their cages. How could she not fall in love with them all?

"Grace, did you hear?" Mom said gently. "Don't get too attached!"

Grace turned back and nodded. She would try....

The rescue shelter wasn't too busy, so Sally took Grace and Danny and Mom around to meet some of the dogs they'd be able to walk. There were so many — Grace was torn between being glad there were lots of dogs for her to get to know, and sad that they all had no homes of their own. It was heartbreaking when the dogs jumped up at the doors of their cages, their tails wagging desperately, licking her fingers, clearly begging for her to love them and take them home.

"Oh, this one's beautiful." Grace knelt down in front of one of the wire-fronted

cages to look at a little brown-and-white Jack Russell. "He's only a puppy!"

Harry looked up hopefully. Grace's voice sounded a little bit like Beth's. But his ears flopped back again when he saw her — just another girl. He turned around in his basket so he didn't have to look at her.

Grace gave him a surprised look. All the other dogs had been desperate for attention, and had wanted all the petting and cuddling they could get. But this little puppy seemed to want them to go away!

"This is Harry," Sally explained. "He's our newest arrival. He was left with us a week ago by a family who were moving to Britain quite suddenly. The girl he belonged to was about your age, Grace. She was really sad to leave him."

"Oh, wow," Grace muttered. She couldn't imagine. Harry looked really young. The other girl couldn't have had him for all that long before she had to give him away.

"He looks pretty miserable," Danny

said, crouching down to get a good look at Harry in his basket.

Sally nodded. "Yes, he's really missing Beth, his old owner. He is eating, but not much, and he won't respond to any of us when we try to cheer him up. I think he's still hoping that Beth's coming back for him."

"That's so sad," Grace said, her voice wobbling. "I wish there was something we could do to help."

Sally looked at her thoughtfully. "Harry isn't ready to go out for walks yet, Grace. If you wanted to spend time with him, it would have to be here at the shelter. Probably just sitting with him in his cage, letting him get used to trusting another person. It's sad, but we just don't have the time for that very often, with so many dogs to take care of."

Grace looked up at Sally, her eyes shining. "But I would love that!" she said gratefully. "Mom, is it okay? Do you mind if I stay here while you and Danny walk your dogs?"

"Well, as long as it's all right with Sally...," Mom said doubtfully.

"Honestly, you'd be doing us a favor," Sally assured them. "We're short-staffed, and we've all been feeling really bad that no one's had time to work with Harry yet. But Grace, don't expect too much to happen at first, okay? It might be a long, slow job. Poor Harry's really moping."

Grace nodded, looking at Harry's smooth little back, as he lay curled into a ball in his basket. His nose was tucked under his paws, as though he was trying to shut out the world. She would take it really slow.

"I'll let you into the cage, then just sit down quietly to start with, not too close to him," Sally told her. "Then I'm afraid it's just all about waiting. See what he does. But if you spend some time with him every time you come, hopefully it will help him. I'll be close to make sure you're both doing okay." She opened the door for Grace, and Grace slipped inside, trying to be as quiet as she could.

Harry raised his head suspiciously and glared at her. It was that girl again. What was she doing in his cage? He huffed angrily through his nostrils, and

Grace tried not to giggle. It was such a funny little noise. She leaned against the wall of the cage and watched Harry, as he turned himself away and snuggled sadly into his basket again. It wasn't quite what she'd imagined, sitting on the floor just looking at a dog, instead of racing around the park. But Harry was so little, and his face when he first looked up at her had been so hopeful, and then so terribly sad. Grace wanted so much for him to be happy again and sat there quietly until her mom and Danny returned.

Harry had always been a friendly dog when he lived with Beth, but he liked his own space, too. He didn't really enjoy being cooped up with a lot of other dogs. And he hated being shut up in a cage. No matter how hard the staff tried to exercise all the dogs, they had to stay in their cages for a lot of the day. As for the noise — Harry was a sensitive little dog, and the sound of barking made him want to hide under his cushion.

What made it worse was that other people kept bothering him. He was taken out of the cage and given to them to hold. He wished they would just leave him alone so he could wait for Beth to come back and get him.

When was she coming back? He was still hoping that she would, but he was getting less sure every day.

That first day, Harry hadn't even looked at Grace. She wanted to go to the rescue shelter on Tuesday, but she had ballet class. But on Wednesday, when Grace visited, Harry actually stood up in his basket and leaned over to give her a considering sniff. Hmm. So it was her again.

On Friday she was back, so he licked her fingers, just to be polite. When she left, he watched her walking down the hallway. She smelled nice, and he wondered if she would come again. On Saturday, he sat up in his basket when she opened the cage, and when she crouched down next to him, he put his paws on her knee, encouraging her to pet him.

"Oh, Harry...." Grace breathed delightedly. He was happy to see her!

Harry hadn't been planning to make friends with the girl, but she was quiet and gentle, and she reminded him of Beth. It was nice to be petted again, and told what a handsome boy he was. He was still waiting for Beth to come back, of course, but there was no harm in letting this nice girl — Grace, the others called her — make a big deal over him.

The next Monday, Sally walked past Harry's cage to see him curled up in Grace's lap while she stroked his ears. Grace was staring down at him with a little smile on her face. She was imagining that Harry was hers, and that they weren't at the rescue shelter; they were sitting on the grass in her yard, a nice big yard, just right for a dog to play in. None of the apartments that they'd seen in their house-hunting had had yards, but this was only a dream, after all....

"You've done really well with him," Sally said, smiling.

Grace jumped slightly — she hadn't noticed Sally coming. Harry grumbled a little when she moved, and turned himself around to get comfy again.

Sally watched him, looking pleased. "You've got a great feeling for animals, Grace. You've been so patient, and it's really paid off with Harry. We'll start trying to introduce him to more visitors now, I think. We'd really like to find a new home for him soon."

Grace only nodded. She couldn't trust herself to say anything. She didn't want Harry to be adopted yet — then she'd never see him again.

Grace frowned at the knitting pattern. She was trying to make a little teddy bear for Harry to have in his basket, but knitting was a lot trickier than it looked when her grandmother did it. She sighed. She had a feeling that it wasn't going to look like the picture, but then Harry would probably chew it to pieces anyway. She just really wanted him to have something to remember her by. Visitors at the shelter kept saying how cute he was, and she was sure he was going to be adopted soon. Grace sniffed, and a tear smudged the crumpled pattern.

"Grace," Danny called around the door. "We've got to go and look at this apartment with Mom and Dad."

Grace frowned. Her room at the

moment was more like a cupboard, but she liked it, even if there wasn't enough space for a desk and she had to do her homework on her bed. It was comfy like that, anyway.

The new apartment was really nice, with a much bigger room for Grace. She could imagine all her dog posters up at last, with all that space, and lots of shelves for her tiny china animals and her books. But it was a second-floor apartment — with no yard.

"So, what did you think?" Dad asked, as they were walking back home. "I really liked it."

Mom nodded. "Me, too. Beautiful kitchen. And your room was great, wasn't it, Grace?"

Grace shrugged.

"What is it?" Dad asked. "Didn't you like it?"

"I'd much rather have a tiny

bedroom, and a yard, so that we could have a dog. I really would. I don't need a big room, honestly."

"She's right," Danny put in. "A yard would be terrific."

Mom sighed. "I know how much you two want a dog, and I've been really impressed with the way you've worked so hard at the rescue shelter. But I still wouldn't feel happy about leaving a dog alone all day. We'll have to think about it."

But she gave Dad a thoughtful look, and leafed through the list of apartments that the real estate agent had given them. Maybe they could find something....

Chapter Three

Harry had started to look forward to Grace's visits. She usually came after school, so at about half-past three he would find himself standing by the door of his cage, sometimes with his paws up on the wire, watching for her. That Friday afternoon, almost two weeks after he'd first met Grace, Harry woke up from a nice snooze in his basket, and stretched out his paws. Now, why had he woken up? Was it time to eat? No.... Ah. It was Grace time. She should be coming to play with him soon.

"Oh, he's adorable! What a beautiful little dog!"

A voice floated over to him, but it didn't sound like Grace. Harry blinked, still a little sleepy, and peered across the cage. A young woman was looking at him, and Sally was with her.

Sally opened the cage to let the woman hold Harry. He allowed her to pick him up, but he kept peering over her shoulder, looking for Grace.

"He's been with us a couple of weeks now. He's a great puppy, but he's been missing his old owner. She had to go overseas. He's cheering up a little now, but any new owners would have to take it slowly with him. Really take the time to build a relationship. And you know that Jack Russells are very energetic? They really need a lot of exercise."

The woman nodded. "I'll definitely go home and talk it over with my husband. I'll let you know very soon."

She waved good-bye to Harry as she walked down the hallway back to the reception area, and Harry wagged his tail delightedly and woofed. The woman smiled, thinking this was all for her — she didn't realize that Grace was just walking through the door behind her. She went home thinking what a sweet, affectionate little dog Harry was. He'd obviously taken to her.

Grace gave the woman a worried look as the door swung shut. Not another person admiring Harry! Everyone who came to the rescue shelter seemed to think he was really cute. Grace had a horrible feeling that Harry would be going to a new home soon.

"Hey, Grace! I'm making some coffee; do you want some juice? And there's a package of chocolate cookies. Would you like one?" Sally waved the package at Grace as she walked past the kitchen on the way to see Harry the next day. On Saturdays Grace usually played with Harry, and then tried to spend some time with any other dogs that the staff thought needed some extra attention. Sally had asked her to help with a couple of other dogs who were quite shy and needed someone patient.

"Chocolate cookies! Yes, please!"

Grace leaned against the kitchen door, nibbling her cookie. She couldn't take it with her, because the dogs would all want to share it, and chocolate wasn't good for dogs.

"You're doing really well with Harry, you know, Grace. It's made a big difference to him, your being here." Sally stirred her coffee thoughtfully. "You're going to miss him when he goes to a new home, aren't you?"

Grace nodded, her mouth full of cookie. "Mmmf."

"Now that he's so much friendlier, I don't think it's going to be all that long before he goes. He's such a sweetie. Just keep it at the back of your mind, okay? I don't want you to be upset, that's all."

Grace stared into her orange juice.

"I know...," she said at last. "I won't be upset. Really." She told herself that it was true, that she'd always known Harry would be adopted. But deep down, she knew that she'd been secretly pretending that he was hers.

"Anyway, I think you could take him for a real walk today, if you'd like to." Sally grinned as Grace nearly hugged her. "Watch it with the juice! I think he's ready. Danny's here, isn't he? Your mom's okay for you to go out if he's with you, isn't she?"

"Yes." Grace nodded excitedly. "I'll tell him."

Sally smiled. "It's okay; I'll find him. You go and put Harry's leash on. He'll be so excited. He just hasn't been getting enough exercise. Jack Russells really like a couple of hour-long walks every day."

Sally was almost right. As soon as Harry saw his leash, he started jumping up wildly, leaping around and practically bouncing off the walls. He could jump easily as high as Grace's waist. She had to pin him under one arm to keep him still enough to put the leash on. "Calm down, calm down, silly boy," she whispered lovingly as he leaped up to try to lick her face.

Eventually she led him proudly out through the reception area, where Danny was waiting with Bella, the Labrador they'd first seen on the rescue shelter website.

It felt so exciting, walking out of the shelter with Harry on his leash — it was a blue one that had been his when he belonged to Beth's family, and he looked wonderful.

"Remember how I showed you the way to keep him under control!" Sally called after them.

Grace looked down at Harry and grinned. Heel was a good idea, but…. He was just so excited. She had to keep gently pulling him back every time he lunged after a strange smell, or wanted to chase a fluttering leaf.

Harry was blissfully happy. He hadn't been outside the shelter in so long — but as soon as he'd seen his leash, and heard Grace say walk, he knew exactly what it meant. He loved walks. He wanted to see everything! Every bee was a possible enemy that needed chasing, every leaf had to be checked out.

Grace was glad that Sally had reminded her to keep a really good hold on Harry when they passed other dogs. A huge German Shepherd was walking along the road toward them, and Harry spotted him even before Grace did. He barked mightily (just to show the German Shepherd he wasn't scared, even if he was a little…) and tried his best to show that he was the bravest, toughest dog in the world.

The German Shepherd's owner smiled at Grace. "You've got a real little character there!"

Grace nodded breathlessly. All her energy was focused on keeping Harry under control. She hoped he wouldn't be like this with every dog in the park!

Luckily, he started to calm down after that, and by the time they were passing the shops, he was walking quite nicely.

"Hey, Grace, if I just tie Bella's leash on this hook, is it okay if I run in and see if they've got the new skateboarding magazine?" Danny asked.

Grace looked doubtfully at Harry. He didn't look like he wanted to stop. "If you're really quick!" she agreed.

"Great. Back in a minute." And

Danny disappeared inside the store. Bella sat down patiently and didn't seem to mind waiting, so Grace bent down to pet Harry.

"Hi, Grace!" Someone was calling. Grace looked around to see her friend Maya from ballet coming down the road with her sister. "I didn't know you had a dog! What's his name? Can I pet him?"

Grace blinked. "His name is Harry," she said slowly. "Yes, of course you can pet him. He's very friendly." She knew she should tell Maya that Harry wasn't actually hers, but she just didn't want to…. It was so nice to pretend that he really belonged to her. Harry was being so good, sitting and letting Maya pat him. Grace was so proud of him! And his good behavior was mostly because of all that time she'd spent with him — so why shouldn't she let Maya think that he was hers?

"Come on, Maya, we've got to go," Maya's sister told her, and Maya stood up reluctantly.

"Grace, could I come over again one day, and play with you and Harry? He's beautiful. You're so lucky!"

Maya had come over to play a couple of times before, and they'd had a great time. But what was Grace supposed to say now? If Maya came over, she'd know that Grace didn't really own Harry.

Grace looked down at the ground. "I'll have to ask my mom," she mumbled.

Luckily, Maya's sister was in a hurry. "Come on, Maya, now!" she said, heading off down the road.

"Um, see you at ballet!" Grace called, as Maya hurried off after her sister.

Maya was calling something back to her, but Grace pretended not to hear. She just hoped Maya didn't think she was being unfriendly. And what was she going to say to her at ballet if Maya asked again about coming over?

Maybe she should have told Maya the truth after all....

Chapter Four

Harry had loved his walk to the park. The only bad thing about it was returning to the shelter. He wished that Grace hadn't brought him back here. He wasn't sure where she went between her visits, but it would be so much nicer if she could take him there with her. She seemed to be sad when they said good-bye, too, so why did she have to leave him behind?

He huddled sadly in the corner of his basket and sighed, wishing that great big dog across the hall would just be quiet. He wanted to go to sleep.

Still, Harry was a lot more cheerful than he'd been before he met Grace. His eyes were brighter, and he played in his cage, instead of being curled up in his basket all day. Everyone admired him now, and Sally was always showing him off to possible owners.

By the next weekend, Grace was starting to get really worried. The other volunteers kept telling her how much people admired him, and she could see that when she was there, too.

"It's lucky that Jack Russells need so much exercise," Grace whispered to Harry, as an elderly lady regretfully went on to look for a less energetic dog. "She really liked you. She'd have taken you if Sally hadn't pointed that out. Oh, I don't believe it, Harry, look. More people!"

A family with a boy a little younger than she was and a baby girl was looking excitedly at Harry.

"I like this one, Daddy!" the boy was saying. "He's great."

The dad looked at Harry running around Grace, and smiled. "He does look nice. Do you work here?" he asked Grace.

Grace nodded. "I volunteer after

school and on the weekends."

"We're looking for a family dog," the mother added. "Do you think that" — she looked at his name card — "Harry would be a good choice?"

Grace gulped. She looked around quickly to check that none of the staff was close enough to hear, then said quietly, "Um, I'm not sure. Jack Russells aren't great with very young children. They can be a little snappy if children bother them too much...."

It was actually true, that Jack Russells could be snappy. But Harry had never shown signs of anything like that, and Grace knew she was being mean by trying to turn them off from Harry. She just couldn't bear to see him go to someone else.

"You might want a gentler dog, with your baby," she added. "Have you seen Maggie? She's a crossbreed, but she's really sweet, and so friendly and well behaved."

Luckily, the family thought Maggie

was beautiful, and when Grace left the rescue shelter, they were talking with Sally about adopting her. But Grace felt terrible all the way home.

"What's up?" Danny asked her. He'd been exercising Bella and Frisky, a retriever, in the outdoor yard. "You haven't told me anything about all the cute stuff Harry did today. Have you managed to get him to shake hands yet? You thought he'd nearly gotten it."

Grace gave a sad little shrug. "He can almost do it. Danny, one of the families who came today really liked him. I sort of turned them off from him, because they had a baby and Jack Russells aren't good with little kids, but it was mostly because I didn't want them to take him…. I don't want him to go," she explained.

"Oh, Gracie," Danny said, putting an arm around her shoulders. "Sally and Mandy warned us when we started. You promised you wouldn't fall in love with any of them."

"I know!" Grace wailed. "But Harry's so beautiful, Danny. I don't want anyone to have him except me!"

Danny sighed. "Well, you managed to turn those people off today, but Gracie, you can't be there every time someone likes him. It's going to happen, you know, sooner or later."

"Some help you are," Grace sniffled, but she knew it was true.

It was about to happen even sooner than Grace had thought. Mrs. Jameson, the young woman who'd asked Sally about Harry, came back that Sunday. She was a perfect owner. No small children, a big yard for him to play in, and she worked from home some of the time so he wouldn't be too lonely. The rescue shelter staff were delighted.

So was Harry. He'd seen Grace come in just after the lady once before, and he assumed they belonged together. So when he saw Sally loading all his toys into his basket, and bringing out his leash for this lady, he was sure that she must be taking him to see Grace. He didn't understand why Grace wasn't coming to get him, but he was sure that that was where they were going.

"What do you think of your new home, Harry?" As Mrs. Jameson put his basket down in the kitchen, Harry looked around with interest. It was nice. Lots of space, and many things to sniff and explore. He wondered where Grace was. He sniffed behind all the cupboards, then checked under the table in case she was hiding. Hopefully she would come soon.

Grace hadn't been able to go to the rescue shelter for a few days. They'd been busy apartment-hunting and today was Tuesday, so she had to go to ballet after school.

She crept into the changing room. Luckily, Mom had dropped her off a little late, so Maya would probably be already changed and in the ballet studio, and Grace wouldn't have to talk to her before the class started. She just knew that Maya was going to ask about Harry, and she still hadn't figured out what to say.

Quickly, Grace changed into her leotard, and put her hair up, then she sneaked into the studio just in time. She looked around for Maya as they did their warm-up routine, but she couldn't see her. All during class, Grace watched for Maya, but she never arrived.

Grace had gotten away with it — for one week, anyway.

Grace ran into the rescue shelter on Wednesday afternoon, dashing ahead of Danny. She'd really missed Harry over the last few days; it felt like forever since she'd seen him. And she'd finally finished Harry's toy last night — she couldn't wait to give it to him.

She ran to Harry's cage, and gasped. He was gone! There was a friendly-looking black spaniel there instead, who woofed an excited hello and came to greet her. Grace stood by the cage, her heart racing, hardly feeling the spaniel licking her fingers.

Maybe he'd been moved? Yes, that was it. Harry must be in one of the other cages, that was all. She said good-bye to the spaniel, who stared after her sadly, and searched the rest of the kennel area. Every cage was full, but none of the dogs was Harry. Sally met her coming in from the outdoor area, her head hanging.

"Oh, Grace! I didn't know you were here yet." Sally looked at her worriedly. "Grace, I'm sorry. I really wanted to tell you before you saw that he was gone."

Grace nodded.

"A really nice lady took him," Sally promised. "She has a big yard for him to run in."

"Oh," Grace whispered. Then she turned and ran back down the hallway.

Danny was putting a leash on one of the other dogs, a big Greyhound that he really liked. He straightened up when Grace brushed past him. "Hey, what's the matter? Grace? Where are you going?" He stared after her, then followed. He had a horrible feeling he already knew what had happened.

Harry lay in his basket, staring sadly around the kitchen. He'd been at his new home for two days now, and his new owners both had to go to work today. He was all alone. He hadn't liked the noise and bustle of the rescue shelter, but it felt very strange for things to be so quiet.

And where was Grace? He had been sure that this was her house and he was going to live with her, but it had been a long time, and she still hadn't come. He was beginning to have a horrible feeling that the wrong person had brought him home, and he didn't know what to do about it.

At least it wasn't dark now. The

kitchen was very scary at night, and he howled for someone to come and keep him company. At Beth's house he had been allowed to sleep on her bed, never shut up on his own all night.

Mrs. Jameson had come downstairs and comforted him the first night, but she wasn't the person he really wanted. Mr. Jameson patted him occasionally, but he kept sniffing, and he sneezed whenever Harry came close to him. His sneezes were very loud, and scary. Harry was spending a lot of time locked in on his own in the kitchen, because he and Mr. Jameson didn't seem to be able to be in the same room together.

Harry sighed. Maybe someone would come and play with him soon.

Maybe even Grace. He really hoped so. But Beth had gone and not come back. Had Grace left him now, too?

Chapter Five

Danny went to the rescue shelter on his own on Thursday. He tried to get Grace to come with him, but she wouldn't. When he got back, he went to her room and tried to cheer her up with funny stories about Finn, his current favorite at the shelter. Finn was half Labrador, half no-one-knew-what, except that he was very big and very hungry. Danny had had to admit to Sally that Finn had found half a packet of mints in his pocket and wolfed them down before Danny could stop him. But luckily, Sally had come to look at Finn, and said she thought it would probably take about six packets of mints to do anything to him; he had an iron stomach.

The story only earned Danny a very small smile. But on Friday after school, he set to work again. "You know, it's not fair on Sally and all the other dogs if you don't go," he pointed out.

"What do you mean?" Grace asked worriedly. She liked Sally a lot; she really didn't want to upset her.

"Well, she's used to having you there to help. If we don't go, the dogs won't get as many walks. I'm taking Finn out again today, but what about Bella and Jake and Harrison? I can't walk all of them, Grace, and not many other people come in to help during the week."

Grace nodded. He was right. It was just hard to imagine going back to the rescue shelter and Harry not being there.

"And don't forget how good everyone at the shelter said you were with the dogs. It'd be a real shame if you stopped going." Danny looked at her hopefully. "Should I call Mom and tell her I'm not dropping you off at home because you're coming with me?" He whipped his cell phone out of his pocket.

Grace sighed. "I suppose so."

"Great!" Danny cheered.

Sally said that Jake really needed a walk, and that Grace and Danny could take him and Finn to the park together.

Grace tried not to be too miserable — it wasn't fair on Jake for a start; he was a beautiful dog, a Westie with a soft white coat. It was difficult, though. She couldn't help remembering the wonderful walk she'd had with Harry.

Finn dragged Danny off to bark at squirrels in the trees on one side of the park, and Grace wandered slowly around the play area with Jake. He was an elderly dog, whose previous owner had died, and he liked gentle walks.

"Grace! Hi!" Someone was calling from the swings, and Grace looked over and saw Maya. Grace smiled and waved at her, but then her smile faded. How was she going to explain Jake?

"Did you miss me at ballet last week?" Maya called, slipping off the swing and running over. "I had a tummy bug, and Mom said if I was missing school, I couldn't go to ballet." Maya looked down at Jake, and then up again, confused. "That's not the same dog you had last time, is it? The other one had a pointier nose."

"Um, yes…," Grace muttered.

"Wow, do you have two dogs now?" Maya asked excitedly.

Grace stared down at Jake and shook her head. She was too embarrassed to look at Maya. "I don't have a dog. They aren't mine. Neither of them." Then she pulled on Jake's leash and suddenly dragged him off across the park.

Maya stood staring after them, looking surprised and a little upset.

Grace found Danny trying to persuade Finn to leave the squirrels alone, and told him what had happened. She was almost crying.

"So you just ran off?" Danny asked in disbelief.

"Yes…," Grace admitted.

"Why didn't you explain? I'll bet she would've understood."

"No, she wouldn't. I'd have to admit that I lied to her when I met her that time with Harry. I let her think he was mine, Danny. I never actually said it, but I didn't tell her he wasn't, either."

Danny blinked as he figured that one out. "I still think she'd understand if you explained it to her. You'll have to at some point anyway. She's bound to ask you at ballet."

"I could stop going to ballet…," Grace suggested desperately.

"Like Mom's going to let you do

78

that! How can you be so good at getting dogs to understand you, but too shy to talk to people?" Danny shook his head. "Nope, you'll just have to explain. Is she still here?"

They looked over at the play area. Maya was there, talking to her sister.

"Come on!" And Danny grabbed Grace's arms and marched her and Finn and Jake across the park.

Grace slowly approached Maya, looking embarrassed.

"Go on," Danny nudged her.

"I'm so sorry," Grace muttered. "I didn't mean to pretend Harry was mine, but when you thought he was, it was so nice. I really, really wanted him to belong to me."

Maya gave her a confused and slightly suspicious look. "So neither of them is yours? Who do they belong to, then?"

Grace sighed sadly. "The animal rescue shelter. Danny and I go and help there after school. We take the dogs for walks."

"Ohhh." Maya nodded.

"I didn't mean to run off. It's just that I suddenly realized you'd know I'd lied to you and I didn't know how to explain everything." Grace looked at Maya hopefully. Danny had been so sure that if she explained, Maya would be okay with it. Was he right?

"If you liked Harry so much, why didn't you take him home?" Maya asked.

"Mom says we can't fit a dog in our

apartment." Grace sighed. "But Harry was so sad when he first came to the shelter. I spent a long time trying to cheer him up, and it was almost like he was mine. When you thought he actually belonged to me, it was like my wish come true."

"At least you can see him at the shelter," Maya said. "It sounds like fun."

Grace sighed. "I can't anymore. Someone else adopted him over the weekend; that's why I have Jake today instead. Harry's gone."

"Oh, Grace! That's so sad." They were silent for a minute, then Maya looked at her shyly. "Do you still go to the rescue shelter? Could I come with you sometime? I love dogs, too; I'd really like to see them all."

"Oh, yes! Why don't you meet us

there tomorrow?" Grace smiled. "Mom said we could definitely go on Saturday morning, didn't she, Danny? And they're always wanting more help."

Grace never even noticed that someone else was there in the park. Mrs. Jameson was working from home, and had taken Harry out for a quick walk. He was enjoying the smells — the park was full of interesting garbage cans, and squirrels, and the scents of other dogs — but he wished he was with Grace. He plodded slowly around the path, watching the other dogs, and the children playing. He wondered where Grace was now.

And then he saw her. Grace was over on the other side of the park — with another dog. Harry stopped in his tracks, and ignored Mrs. Jameson gently pulling on his leash. Had she forgotten him already? Harry barked and barked, pulling on his leash as hard as he could, but she was too far away to hear him. Did Grace have another dog now? He missed her so much, as much as he'd missed Beth when she went away. Why did everyone go away? Harry sat down in the middle of the path and howled broken-heartedly.

Mrs. Jameson was worried that he might be hurt somehow. She picked him up and hurried home, where he curled up in his basket and didn't want to play all evening. He even refused to eat. He felt so lonely, and he wanted Grace to come back for him so much. Why did she have another dog now? Didn't she love him anymore?

Mrs. Jameson didn't know what was wrong with Harry, and when her husband got home from work, she told him how upset Harry seemed. "I want him to be happy here, but he doesn't seem to be settling in at all," she admitted.

Mr. Jameson sighed. "I'm not sure this is working out, either...."

Mrs. Jameson nodded sadly. "I know.

We can't just keep shutting Harry in the kitchen, and your allergy's getting worse every day."

Mr. Jameson gave her a hug. "I'm sorry. I know you really wanted a dog...."

His wife smiled. "But it isn't fair on either of you. I'll call the rescue shelter tomorrow and arrange to take him back." She sniffed. "Poor little Harry...."

Chapter Six

Maya and her sister were waiting outside the rescue shelter for Grace when Grace and Danny and Mom arrived on Saturday afternoon. Maya was going to stay for a couple of hours, and then her sister was coming back to pick her up. Grace was delighted to have someone to show around, and Maya loved meeting all the dogs.

They were just saying hello to Jake, the Westie, when Grace heard a familiar yap from the next cage. She turned slowly to look. Could it be....

"Harry!" Grace cried, and he bounded up to the door of the gate, leaping and barking delightedly.

"Oh, it's really you! What are you doing back here?" Grace asked, petting him through the wire.

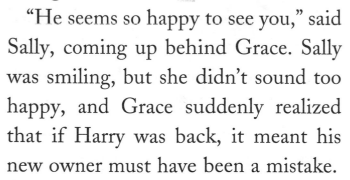

"He seems so happy to see you," said Sally, coming up behind Grace. Sally was smiling, but she didn't sound too happy, and Grace suddenly realized that if Harry was back, it meant his new owner must have been a mistake.

"Did the people not want him after all?" she asked, gazing fondly at Harry.

Sally sighed. "Harry didn't settle in very well, unfortunately. I'm sure he would have been fine over time, but the husband turned out to be allergic to dogs, too. Poor Harry. Back here again, aren't you, sweetheart?"

Grace looked at Harry lovingly. She slipped into his cage and sat down, letting him climb all over her. She was so glad to see him again. But then a horrible thought struck her. Harry hadn't settled at his new home — was that her fault? Because she'd been spending so much time with him? If he was too fond of her, he might not want to go to a new owner.

"What's the matter?" Maya asked.

"Aren't you happy he's back?"

Grace sighed. "I am happy. But Sally said he didn't settle in at his new home. What if that's because he's spending too much time with me?"

Maya looked confused, and Grace tried to explain. "He's going to be adopted again. What if I spoil another new home for him? Maybe I just shouldn't see him anymore."

Harry lay blissfully in Grace's lap, his paws folded on his stomach, eyes closed. The only thing that could make this better would be some food. He was fairly sure dinner would be here soon….

"Harry…. Harry…." Grace was whispering to him. "I have to go, sweetie. It's time for you to eat." She lifted him gently off her lap.

Harry slid off sleepily, and looked up at her, puzzled. She was going? Again? But she'd only just come back! Grace was opening the door of his cage, and he flung himself at her, howling. No! He didn't want her to go. She might not come back again!

Grace shut the door of the cage, her fingers trembling. Harry was howling so loudly that everyone in the rescue shelter was looking around, wondering what was happening.

Sally walked quickly toward them. "Don't worry, Grace. I've got some food for him; hopefully that'll help calm him down. You go. See you soon, okay? Don't worry about Harry. He's just had a hard couple of days."

Grace nodded, blinking back tears. It was really hard to leave him when he was so upset. Maya and Danny were hurrying up the hallway toward her, looking worried.

"Maya told me Harry was back. Was that him howling?" Danny asked.

Grace nodded and sniffed. Danny gave her a hug and they headed for the door. Mom was waving to them from the reception area, telling them to hurry up.

Maya had just opened the door when there was a sudden crash, and they turned back to see that Sally had dropped Harry's food bowl. It looked like he'd jumped at the door of the cage

as she'd opened it, and run into her.
Now he was racing between the cages,
barking madly, with Sally chasing after
him.

Harry settled at Grace's feet, his
tail wagging desperately. Other people
were allowed to take him home. Why
couldn't she? She was the one he
wanted to go home with!

Hopefully, he held out one paw,
the way she'd been teaching him.
Grace's eyes were full of tears as she
crouched down to take it. Harry gave
a triumphant little bark. He'd done it
right. There. Surely she couldn't send
him back to his cage now.

Grace picked him up, and rubbed
her cheek against his smooth fur. Then
she handed him back to Sally, and ran.

She couldn't bear to see him like this.

Danny, Maya, and Mom found her outside the rescue shelter, leaning against the wall and crying.

"Oh, Grace…," Mom said worriedly. "I'm sure he'll be all right in a minute." Grace gave her a disbelieving look, and Mom sighed. "Well, maybe not right away, but I'm sure he will get over it."

"But it isn't fair!" Grace sobbed. "He's always having to get over things. His first owner had to leave him, and now this one's given up on him, and he just wants to be with me and I can't have him!"

Mom put an arm around her shoulders comfortingly, and Danny asked, "Mom, isn't there any way we could have him? You know how hard Grace has worked."

"I do know, and I'm really proud of you, Grace. But Harry needs a lot of space to run around. And he'd hate being shut in his cage while we're all out during the day. I'm sorry, Grace; I wish things were different, but you know we can't have a dog at the moment."

Chapter Seven

"He's as bad as he was when he first came," Mandy said sadly, looking at the little brown-and-white ball in the basket. It was all they'd been able to see of Harry for days.

Sally called gently, "Harry! Here, boy!" but he didn't even twitch. "It's so sad. He really adored Grace, but I can understand why she doesn't think she should visit him anymore, and it's probably for the best."

"Still, there's a family coming to see him this afternoon," said Mandy. "They saw him on the website, and they think he looks perfect. If they like him, and they can give him the time to settle in...."

They stared at Harry, still curled up silently, and Sally sighed. "Well, you never know...."

Grace didn't go to the rescue shelter at all that week. She just couldn't bear it. She had made Harry's life even harder by falling in love with him. He had to find a new home, and she was stopping him.

She just had to let him go, and the sooner, the better.

She supposed she could have gone back to the shelter and kept away from Harry, but that would be so difficult. Danny didn't even try to persuade her this time. Mom had called the shelter to talk to Sally and explain. Grace had listened to what Mom was saying, and she could tell that Sally was sad, but that she agreed with Mom. It was the best thing for Harry.

Life was very boring without the rescue shelter to go to, though, Grace thought, lying on her bed listening to her favorite CD. School, more school, hanging around at home. She'd gone to Maya's to play yesterday, which was nice, but she still missed Harry, and all the other dogs, so much.

"Grace!" Mom called from the kitchen. "Time to go!"

Grace sighed, and rolled off her bed. Another apartment to go and see.

Grace smiled politely as Sheila, the lady who owned the apartment, chatted to her about whether she liked the bedroom that would be hers. She just wished Mom and Dad would stop fussing about the bathroom and get going; she was so sick of apartment-hunting. They'd already seen this apartment anyway, yesterday, when Grace and Danny were at school. Why did they need to look at everything again?

They finished at last, and Sheila led them back toward the kitchen. "I'll just show you the yard," she said over her shoulder. "I cleaned it up a bit since you saw it yesterday, but I'm afraid I'm not much of a gardener."

Grace gasped. "A yard! There's a yard?"

Sheila turned back and smiled. "Yes. Didn't your parents tell you? The yard goes with this ground-floor apartment."

Grace looked at Mom and Dad, her eyes wide with hope. "So could we…?"

Mom nodded and laughed. "Yes! I mean, it'll take a little while before we can move in, of course. But your dad and I have talked this over, and yes, we can have Harry."

Grace flung herself at her mom and

hugged her. "You planned all this. I can't believe it!"

Her mom laughed and led her over to the window. "When we saw it, we realized how perfect it would be for you and Danny. You've both worked so hard at the rescue shelter. Now you get to have your own dog."

They looked out at the yard. It was messy, full of weeds, but Grace could just imagine Harry bounding up and down, barking joyfully as she threw a ball for him to chase.

Danny stared out, too, his face split by an enormous grin, but then he frowned. "What about us all being out in the daytime? You said we couldn't leave Harry alone all day."

Dad nodded. "It's okay. I've spoken to my bosses, and they're fine with me bringing Harry into the office some of the time. And when I have meetings, your mom should be able to stop home and give him a walk during her lunch hour."

"Oh, Dad!" Grace hugged him, and then her mom again. "Thank you so much! Can we go home and call the shelter now?"

When they got back, Grace was standing hopefully holding the phone before anyone else had even gotten their coat off. She'd even found the number on the kitchen bulletin board.

"All right, all right!" Mom laughed and took the phone.

Grace waited with her fingernails digging into her palms, listening to the ringing on the other end.

"Oh, hello. Could I speak to Sally, please? Oh, it's you, Sally. This is Amanda Winter, Grace and Danny's mom. Yes, we're all fine, thank you. We've missed you, too. But actually, we've got some good news. We're moving, and we're going to have more space in our new apartment. We think we might be able to adopt Harry after all." Mom smiled excitedly at Grace, but then there was a long pause, and the smile faded. Her voice had flattened when she next spoke. "Oh. Oh, I see. Yes, well, that's good. Yes. We should have expected it. I'll tell her. Thanks. Bye."

"Someone else has taken him, haven't they?" Grace asked, her voice shaking, and Mom nodded.

"Oh, Gracie, I'm so sorry." She sighed. "Sally said he's gone to a family this time. The children aren't too young for a dog, and they're all excited to have him. He'll have a wonderful time...." But she couldn't make the words sound happy.

"If only we'd found the apartment sooner!" Grace wailed.

"It's terrible luck," Mom agreed. "We'll just have to try and be happy for Harry. I know it's hard."

Dad picked up Grace and hugged her, even though he was always saying she was too big for him to do that now. Danny sat at the kitchen table with his chin on his hands, staring out the window. "I can't believe we just missed him," he muttered. "It isn't fair...."

"You probably don't want to think about this right now," Dad said slowly. "But — there are other dogs. Lots of dogs at the shelter who need a home."

"Not yet," Grace interrupted. "We couldn't just yet."

"No, I know. But think about it. Harry's found a nice home. But we could give a good home to another dog."

Grace nodded, and sniffed. At last she said slowly, "Maybe. We could have Finn. He's your favorite, isn't he, Danny? The one who ate your mints?" Her voice was shaking.

Danny nodded. "But I think he's too big, even for an apartment with a yard. Harry would have been perfect...."

"He would, wouldn't he?" Grace tried to smile. "I suppose at least now I can go and help at the rescue shelter again, without worrying about upsetting Harry. Oh, I hope he likes the new people! He deserves a better chance this time!"

Chapter Eight

It was a little more than a week later, and Grace was sitting in her new bedroom. It was much bigger than her old one, but she hadn't finished unpacking her things yet. She just couldn't summon the energy. Mom kept telling her to get going, but Grace couldn't help stopping to look out her window, imagining Harry playing out there. If she half-closed her eyes, she could almost see him, hiding under that big bush, getting ready to leap out at her....

Grace rubbed her hand across her eyes. Harry had a new home now. It was a nice family, Sally had said, when she went back to help at the shelter. He would be over the moon, with so many people to love him. The

tears started to run down her cheeks again as she pictured him, curled up on a bed just like this one, while a girl the same age as her petted him gently.

Harry was pulling anxiously at his leash as Sam Ashcroft coaxed him to chase the ball. The children were so bouncy and excited, and it was just too much for him. Harry had had such a hard time recently — moving around all over the place, and having to get used to so many new people. He simply wasn't ready for three energetic children who wanted him to play all the time.

"Why won't he chase it?" Sam asked angrily. "I've been trying forever."

"Maybe he's tired," Luke suggested. "Mom's over there talking to that lady from school. We'd better tell her."

"But I don't want to go home!" Lily wailed, and Harry flinched at the noise.

Mrs. Ashcroft said good-bye to her friend and walked over to the children. "Come on, guys, we need to get home. Sally from the rescue shelter is coming to see how we're doing with Harry."

Harry plodded along the pavement with Luke, jumping when cars whooshed past. Everything seemed scary at the moment. He wished he could just curl up in his basket, and everyone would leave him alone. His ears were tensely pricked for the entire walk, and when a piece of litter blew in front of him, he gave a sharp, frightened little bark.

Mrs. Ashcroft looked at him worriedly, but she didn't say anything.

The children were even noisier than usual when they got home. After Lily had nearly run him over twice with her doll's stroller, Harry decided to take drastic action. He hid under the sofa. It was quiet, it was dark, and nobody could find him to make him chase balls, or jump into boxes, or even just hug him. He didn't want to be hugged right now.

The doorbell rang, and Harry shuddered as the children thundered down the hallway to the door.

"I just don't know where he could've gone," Mrs. Ashcroft was saying worriedly. "We came back from our walk about 20 minutes ago. He must have slipped away somewhere."

"Is he settling in well?" It was a familiar voice. Harry was sure he knew it. It wasn't Grace, but it made him think of her. He poked his nose out from under the sofa to hear better.

"There he is!" Lily shrieked, and Harry shot backward.

Lily crouched down to peer under the sofa, and Harry backed away from her. She swept her hand underneath, and called to him to come out. Harry barked anxiously. Why wouldn't they just leave him alone?

"Lily, stop that!" Mrs. Ashcroft said worriedly. "Now, Lily!"

Harry was still barking, a sharp, unhappy bark that sounded like a warning. *Leave me alone! Go away!*

Lily scrambled to her feet, her bottom lip wobbling. "I don't like it when he barks like that," she said tearfully.

Mrs. Ashcroft sighed, and looked at Sally. "I was hoping to be able to tell you he was starting to settle in," she said. "But I just don't think he is. The children have tried really hard, but I think we're a bit too much for him to take. He's a wonderful little dog, but he just doesn't seem very happy."

Sally nodded sadly. "I think you're right. I have a dog carrier in my car. I'm so sorry it hasn't worked out.

Hopefully we can find you another dog — one that's used to a busy house."

Mrs. Ashcroft and the children left Sally to coax Harry out, which she managed to do by being very quiet, and opening a package of dog treats.

Then it was back to the animal rescue shelter — again.

"He really is the boomerang dog, isn't he?" Sally sighed, as she and Mandy watched Harry eating his breakfast on Sunday morning.

"It's such a shame Grace couldn't take him home," Mandy said. "She built up such a wonderful relationship with him."

Sally nodded, then she smiled slowly.

"Of course! You've given me a great idea! I wonder if Grace and Danny are coming in today. I'm going to give their mom and dad a call."

She came back out of the reception area smiling. "They'll be here shortly. I can't wait to see Grace's reaction."

Mandy was frowning. "But I thought you'd decided that Harry loving Grace so much was keeping him from settling in with a new owner. Are you sure you want him to see her again?"

Sally nodded. "But I didn't tell you — the family moved. They wanted to adopt Harry, but he'd already gone to the Ashcrofts. They were going to think about another dog when they felt ready. And I've told them that the perfect dog has just arrived...."

Grace pushed open the door to the dogs' area, leading the way for Mom and Dad and Danny. Her hands felt sweaty, and slipped on the door handle. She was so nervous. Sally had said that a wonderful new dog had arrived, one who would be perfect for Grace and her family.

Why wasn't she happy?

All she could think of was Harry. She tried desperately to picture him with those other children, having a wonderful time. This other dog really needed a home, too.

"You all right?" Danny asked her, looking at her thoughtfully.

"I suppose," Grace whispered. "It just feels odd."

"I know." He sighed. "But this dog will be great, too."

Grace grabbed his arm. "Look!"

Sally was walking down the hallway, carrying a puppy in her arms. A Jack Russell puppy, white with brown patches, whose ears pricked up when he heard Grace's voice. He gave one joyful bark, and twisted right out of Sally's hold, leaping to the ground, his paws scratching the floor frantically as he raced toward them.

"Harry! It's Harry!" Grace scooped him up, and he licked her face delightedly, then generously leaned out of her arms to lick Danny, too. He'd missed Grace so much, and she'd come — she'd come back for him!

Sally grinned. "Told you I had the perfect dog...."

"I can't believe it," Grace whispered, hugging Harry tightly. "Thank you so much!" she told Sally.

Sally smiled at her. "I'm just glad he's found the right home at last. I don't think he'll be coming back to us again. But you have to do me one favor. Will you write to Beth, his old owner, for me? Tell her all about Harry's new home?"

"Of course!" Grace nodded eagerly.

Harry looked around to see Sally getting his basket and toys out of the cage and handing them to Danny. She gave Grace his leash. Harry's stubby little tail wagged delightedly as Grace clipped on the leash. He'd never seen Grace look this happy before. He gave her a hopeful look. If his basket and his toys were coming....

Grace was staring at him with shining eyes. "Oh, Harry! You're really coming home with us. We don't have to say good-bye this time."

"Harry, don't chew that pencil," Grace giggled. "Dogs aren't meant to eat pencils. It's not good for you."

She reached over to her nightstand. "Here — have a dog biscuit instead. But don't leave any crumbs on the comforter, okay? Mom's not sure about your being on my bed; we don't want to give her anything to complain about!"

Harry gnawed happily on the dog biscuit, letting Grace chat away. He loved it when she talked to him. Maybe after she'd finished this thing she was doing they could go to the park, with Danny, too. He gulped the last of the bone, and stretched out his paws. She was still writing. He'd take a little nap.

Grace looked down at him lovingly, curled up next to her teddy bear. She couldn't believe Harry had found a home at last — with her.

Dear Beth,

Sally gave me your address so I could write and tell you all about Harry. He has been living with us for two weeks now, and he is wonderful. (I know you know that already!) I really hope you're enjoying living in London, and you don't miss him too much.

Did Harry like smoky bacon treats when he lived with you? He stole a whole packet out of my brother's bag yesterday. Luckily Danny loves him so much that he went and got him another packet from the store. Mom was really angry, but it's okay — Harry wasn't sick.

Harry loves playing in our yard and going for walks, and he's very good at doing tricks now. He can shake hands, and roll over, and he'll almost stay, but not if you put a dog biscuit in front of him. We're still working on that one!

Lots of love,
Grace and Harry

Out Now:

Fluff, a barn cat, is desperate to find a home of her own like her brothers and sisters. Sadly, no one seems to want her….

Then a little girl named Ella comes to the farm where Fluff lives. Ella falls in love with Fluff immediately and begs her mother to let her have the kitten. But her mother says no — they don't want a cat.

Fluff and Ella are heartbroken…and Fluff is terrified. What happens to kittens that nobody wants?

HOLLY
WEBB

Holly Webb started out as a children's book editor, and wrote her first series for the publisher she worked for. She has been writing ever since, with more than 90 books to her name. Holly lives in England with her husband and three young sons. She has three pet cats, who are always nosing around when Holly is trying to type on her laptop.

For more information
about Holly Webb visit:

www.holly-webb.com
www.tigertalesbooks.com